The Secret Hide-out

Story and pictures by JOHN PETERSON

SCHOLASTIC BOOK SERVICES
NEW YORK · TORONTO · LONDON · AUCKLAND · SYDNEY · TOKYO

To my son Matt,

the Founder and President

of the Viking Club of Primrose Farm

A hardcover edition of this book is published by Four Winds Press,
a division of Scholastic, and is available through your local bookstore
or directly from Four Winds Press, 50 West 44th Street, New York,
N.Y. 10036.

Copyright © 1965 by John Peterson. Published by Scholastic Book Services, a division of
Scholastic Magazines, Inc.

18 17 16 15 14 13 12 11 10 9 8   5 6 7 8 9/7 0/8

Printed in the U.S.A.

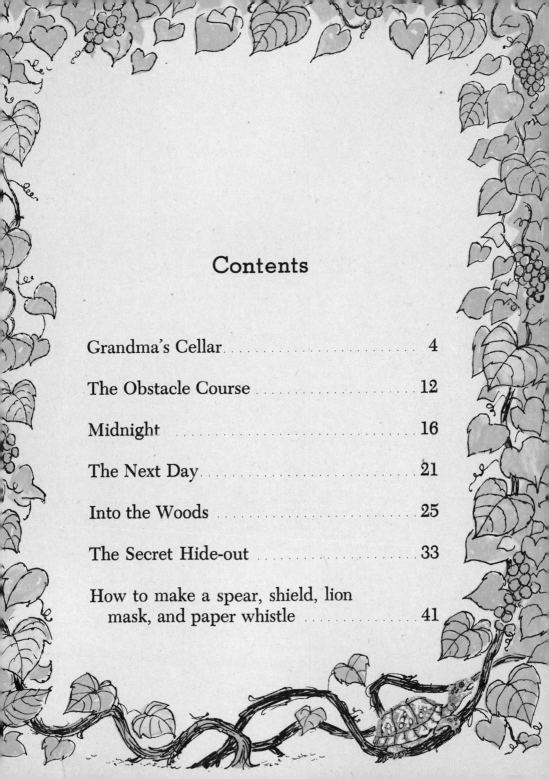

Contents

Grandma's Cellar

"Pull! Pull harder. It's got to come out," said Sam.

"I'm pulling as hard as I can," said Matt.

The boys were standing in a dark cellar. Matt Burns was pulling at a stone in the wall. His younger brother, Sam, was holding a flashlight so he could see.

Suddenly the loose stone gave way. "Ooooops!" said Matt. He fell backward and bumped into his brother. They both fell down.

Matt jumped to his feet. He grabbed the flashlight away from Sam. He pointed it at the hole in the wall. "There — see? I told you. There's something behind that stone."

Sam stuck his hand in the hole. "Ick!" he said. "Cobwebs! I can't stand cobwebs."

"For Pete's sake, they can't hurt you," said his brother. He reached deep into the cellar wall. "Hey! I got hold of some papers or something."

"Let's see!" said Sam.

Matt pulled the mysterious papers out of the hole. "Hey! It's a notebook."

"Look, it has gold words on the cover," said Sam. "What does it say?"

"I can't read it," said Matt. "Wait until I get this dust off." He brushed away the dirt with his shirt sleeve. The gold letters sparkled:

The secret book of the VIKING CLUB 1938

"What does it mean?" said

"Gee!" said Matt, "it lo

Viking Club back in 19

club book. Somebody

Grandma's cellar years and

"Before we were born, even,

They opened the book. Matt read

aloud:

JUNIOR MEMBERS, ATTENTION!

This is the one and only super-secret book of the mighty Viking Club. Don't tell anybody at all where this secret book is hidden. If you do, you will get the supreme penalty.

Also, don't tell what you have seen in the book. This book has all the membership tests in it. Do ALL the tests. You will become a SENIOR member if you can pass the tests.

Only senior members can come to the secret hide-out. When you come to the secret hide-out, you take the oath of membership. Then you will be a member forever. Good luck.

mackerel!" said Sam. "A secret hide-out!
ee if we can find it. Where does it tell about
ecret hide-out?" He reached for the book.

Wait — look at this," said Matt turning the page.
These guys had code names and everything. See?"
He showed the page to his brother.

President — GOLDEN TIGER
Vice President — RED FEATHER
First Scout — SCREAMING EAGLE
Secretary — SPOTTED HORN

"I'm Golden Tiger, I'm Golden Tiger," said Sam.
He jumped up and down.

"That's what *you* think," said Matt. "Golden Tiger
was the president, and you're *not* the president. We
all have to make up our own secret name."

"Then I choose Star Fire," said Sam.

"I have a great idea for a name," said Matt. "I'll
be Black Hawk. Hawks fly faster than anything."

"What's next?" said Sam. "This book is keen."

Matt turned the page. "Wow! Look at this! Look
at this obstacle course."

"What's that?" said Sam. "What's an obstacle course?"

"It's something like running a race," said Matt, "and there are things you have to crawl under or jump over. Here's how it works." He pointed to the picture in the secret book.

"First you hop into this automobile tire. Then you run and touch the garage doors.

"After that you crawl through this box. But don't knock the ball off the box, see?

"Then you run around these milk bottles. And don't knock them over either.

"Then you jump over this string that's tied between these two trees — hey!" He jabbed his finger at the book. "Those trees — that's an elm and the other is a pine tree. See? Just like the two trees near Grandma's garage. They must have used Grandma's back yard for the tests."

"Let's set it up! I'll bet we can run around their old obstacle course just as fast as they could," said Sam.

"O.K., but we will have to use milk cartons. I don't think Grandma Burns gets milk bottles any more," said his brother.

"Wait!" said Sam. "First we have to promise not to tell anyone about the book. Right?"

"O.K., but we have to tell Beany," said Matt. "He'll find out anyway. He's always hanging around."

"Just Beany, though," said Sam. "Nobody else. Right?"

"Right," said Matt. "But later on we can let some of the kids be junior members."

"Come on, let's go. Let's make the obstacle course. I can run through it easy," said Sam.

"Yeah, but don't forget — we have to run through it three times without a mistake," said Matt.

"I'll bet I can do it ten times," said his brother.
"Oh, cut it out. Stop showing off," said Matt. "You
get Beany. I'll see if that old tire is still in the brook."

The Obstacle Course

LATER IN THE DAY, Matt and Sam stood in the back yard and watched Beany. He was zigzagging through the milk cartons.

"Watch where you're running," said Matt.

Beany's foot hit a milk carton. It almost fell over. He stopped and looked back.

"Come on, Beany! Make that one last jump," said Sam.

"You guys did it — I can do it," said Beany. He ran on toward the high jump.

Matt held his breath. Sam closed his eyes.

Beany jumped . . .

Snap! went the string.

"I knew it, I knew it," said Matt.

"Aw, I fell over my shoelace," said Beany.

"Well, the next time try to get off the ground, will you?" said Matt.

"I'd like to see you jump with *your* shoelace untied," said Beany.

"Tie the string together, Sam," said Matt. "This is the last time, Beany. We're running out of string."

"Try real hard, Beany. You've got to do it this time or you won't get in the club," said Sam.

Beany tied his shoelaces. He looked at the string. Then he ran slowly toward the string. As he leaped he yelled, "Geronimo o o o o o o!"

Sam cheered, "Hey, Beany — that's great!"

"You went up like a rocket," said Matt. He patted Beany on the back.

"I think it was the yell that did it," said Sam. "I think that yelling helped him."

"What's the next test?" said Beany.

Matt read from the book. "Every member has to sleep out all night. He must lie down under the oak tree in the yard. At midnight he must try to kill the monster with a spear."

"Monster!" cried Beany. "Are you kidding? What monster?"

"It must be a joke or something," said Sam.

"If it's in the book, I think we should do it," said Matt.

"How do we get spears?" said Beany.

"It tells how to make them in the book," said Matt. "Shields, too. You've got to have a shield."

"Why?" said Beany.

"Suppose the monster attacks us," said Matt. "Don't you know anything, Beany? Here — look at this plan." He held the book up for them to see. "The spear is made from a broomstick. And the shield from a bushel-basket lid. Isn't it great?"

"We can get some paint from Grandma to paint the shields," said Sam. "I'm going to paint a shooting star on mine."

"I'm going to paint a dragon on mine," said Beany.

"Wait until you see my black hawk," said Matt. "I can draw a wonderful hawk."

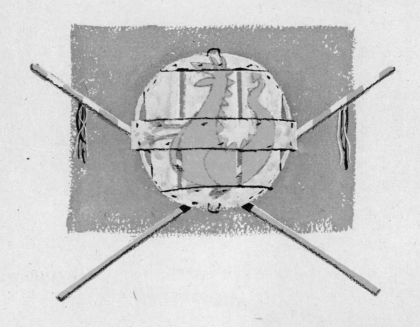

Midnight

THAT NIGHT the moon was round and bright. Strange shadows filled the yard. The boys were lying in sleeping bags under the oak tree. At first they heard nothing.

"It's so quiet, it's spooky," said Beany.

Then they began to hear the night sounds. A hum of crickets came from the grass. They heard the wind in the leaves. An owl hooted.

"Why do owls have to sound so sad?" said Sam.

"What's that?" said Beany. "What's making that squeaking noise?"

They listened.

"It's nothing," said Matt. "That's just two old branches of a tree rubbing together."

"Gee," said Beany. "Do you suppose there really is a monster?"

"Boy, I hope so," said Sam. "I want to try this spear. She's a beauty."

"Hey, let's be quiet, you guys," said Matt. "It's time to go to sleep."

"Hey, Beany, wake up!" Matt whispered.

"W-w-what, what's the matter?" said Beany.

"It's midnight," said Matt. "Time to kill the monster."

"What monster?" Beany yawned.

"You know — the monster. The test in the secret book, remember?"

"Oh yeah, I forgot. Is Sam awake?"

"He's already on the lookout. Come on, follow me. And don't forget your spear."

Matt and Beany crawled through the grass. They saw Sam standing in the moonlight. He was waving his shield and pointing with his spear.

"Look, over there — by the fence. Something is moving," said Beany.

"Get down, Sam, get down!" said Matt. "It may attack."

Sam fell to the ground. Matt ran to him.

Beany pointed toward the fence. "Wowee! There really *is* a monster!"

"This is it!" Matt cried. "Let's get him!" He threw his spear. It whistled through the air.

Sam jumped to his feet. "Come on, Beany — let's get him!"

Sam and Beany threw their spears as hard as they could.

"We got him! We got him!" Matt shouted.

Nothing moved. Even the leaves were silent for a moment.

"He's dead for sure," said Beany. "Come on, let's go back to sleep."

"We have to make sure we got him," said Sam.

"I wouldn't go over there for anything," said Beany. "He may be only wounded."

"Are you kidding?" said Sam. "You just said he was dead."

"I think we should wait until daylight," said Matt. "Besides, we don't have any more spears."

"Yeah," said Beany. "You'd have to be crazy to go after a wounded monster without a spear."

The Next Day

MATT WOKE FIRST the next morning. He sat up and looked toward the fence. "The monster is gone!" he yelled. "Get up, you guys."

"I told you we should have made sure," said Sam. "Now it's gone."

The three boys ran to the fence. They found their spears stuck in a bush.

"Darn it! I really thought we'd got him," said Matt.

"I guess we scared him away," said Beany.

Matt pulled his spear out of the bush. "Boy! If this was his head, I would have got him right between the eyes."

A bell rang behind them.

"The breakfast bell," Matt yelled. He ran toward the house.

"Come on, Beany — pancakes!" said Sam. "I'll race you to the door."

Grandma Burns had plenty of pancakes ready for them when they got to the kitchen. "Wipe your feet before you come in. And wash your hands before you sit down," she said.

"What's the next test?" said Sam. His mouth was full of pancakes.

"Don't talk with your mouth full, Sammy dear. Your father wouldn't like that," said Grandma.

"It's a lion mask," said Matt. "We have to make it out of a paper bag. All Viking Club members have to wear lion masks."

"Would you like another pancake, Beany?" said Grandma.

"Yes, thank you!" said Beany.

"And look at this paper whistle," said Matt. He held up the book so Sam could see. "You blow the whistle and give your code name. That's the signal to get into the hide-out."

"A lion mask and a whistle!" shouted Sam. "Boy! Those guys thought of everything."

"Please, boys. Don't shout at the table," said Grandma. She smiled at Sam and patted his head.

"Come on, men," said Matt. "Let's get to work on this test."

"What test?" said Mr. Burns. Matt and Sam's father came into the room. "I thought we were on a vacation. Why are you taking tests?"

"Aw, it's nothing, Dad. We're just having fun," said Matt. He hid the book behind his back.

"What's that?" said Mr. Burns. "That book. It looks like —"

"It's kind of a secret," said Matt. He backed up toward the door.

"Well, make sure your secret doesn't get you into any trouble. Remember, we're visitors here. We have to behave ourselves, or Grandma will send us home."

"We will, Dad," said Matt. He turned the door knob. Sam slipped through the open door.

"Don't worry, Mr. Burns," Beany said. "We're just having fun."

They ran into the yard.

"I hope they had enough to eat," said Grandma Burns. She closed the door after them.

Into the Woods

Matt and Sam finished their lion masks first. Beany worked a little longer on his mask.

"Try it on, Beany," said Matt. "Let's see."

Beany put on his mask.

"Hey! That's great! Doesn't he look real scary?" said Sam.

"Give us the signal," said Matt. "Blow the whistle and call out your code name."

Beeeeep! Beany blew his whistle. "Red Dragon."

"Good," said Matt. "Let's hear it, Sam."

Beeeeep! Sam blew loudly. "Star Fire."

"O.K. men!" said Matt. "Let's go find the secret hide-out."

"Where is it?" said Beany.

"We follow this map in the secret book," said Matt. "First we have to find a big rock near the brook."

The boys headed for the woods. Matt was in front. "Don't stay too close together. We may get ambushed," he said.

"Let's keep off the paths," said Sam. "Somebody might follow us."

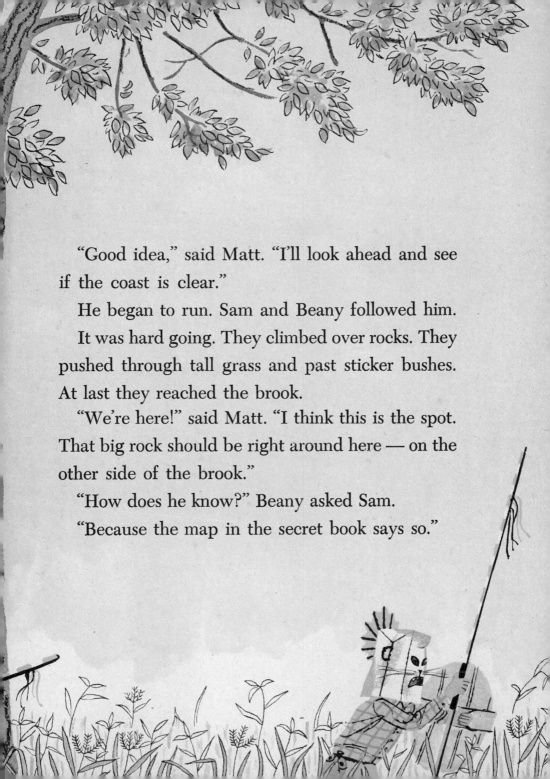

"Good idea," said Matt. "I'll look ahead and see if the coast is clear."

He began to run. Sam and Beany followed him.

It was hard going. They climbed over rocks. They pushed through tall grass and past sticker bushes. At last they reached the brook.

"We're here!" said Matt. "I think this is the spot. That big rock should be right around here — on the other side of the brook."

"How does he know?" Beany asked Sam.

"Because the map in the secret book says so."

"But that was years and years ago. It's probably not in the same place."

Sam looked at Beany. "Big rocks like that don't move around, Beany. They don't have legs."

"Hey, fellows, come here!" shouted Matt. "I think I've found it."

Sam and Beany climbed over the wet, slippery rocks.

"Look at this," said Matt. He was standing near a very large rock. "Do you see these two little holes in this rock? I'm going to put a small stick in each hole, like this. Then we can look from one stick to the other to see the right direction. It's just like aiming a gun."

"What do you see?" said Benny.

"Just that dumb bush there," said Matt.

"Maybe that bush wasn't there when the map was made," said Sam.

"I'll bet you're right," said Matt. "Bend the bush over, will you? And I'll look past it."

Sam and Beany grabbed the top of the bush. They pulled it to the ground. Now Matt could see past it easily.

"What do you see?" Beany asked again.

Matt looked across the two sticks. "There it is!" he yelled. "I'll bet anything that's it."

"Where?" said Sam.

"There — on the side of the hill, see? The old grapevine — just like the book says. We've found it! We've found it!"

"Yipee!" yelled Sam. He let go of the bush. It snapped up and knocked Beany over.

"Now why did you go and do that?" Beany whined.

"Come on — last one to the hide-out is a monkey," said Sam.

"Hold it!" said Matt. "We have to sneak up on it. Suppose somebody's watching?"

"Who?" said Beany, surprised.

"I don't know who," said Matt. "But it's a secret hide-out, isn't it? How are we going to keep it a secret if we go walking up to it in broad daylight like it was somebody's house or something?"

"My brother is right," said Sam. "We have to crawl up there."

"I guess you're right. But that sure is a long way," said Beany.

Matt swung his shield onto his back. "O.K., let's go," he said. He threw himself flat on the ground. He held his spear in front of him and began to crawl. Sam and Beany crawled behind him.

The Secret Hide-out

THEY SNEAKED through the grass like three strange snakes. High in the sky the sun seemed to follow them. It felt warm on their backs.

Beany sneezed...

"Quiet! You'll give away our position!" Matt whispered.

"I can't help it," Beany giggled. "This grass tickles my nose."

"Everybody stop!" Matt hissed. "The ground is wet here — kind of swampy."

"Can we crawl through it?" said Sam.

"Naw — it's too wet," said Matt.

"Then let's run through it," said Beany, "and attack the hide-out."

"Beany, are you coocoo or something? Why should we attack our own hide-out?" said Matt.

"I just thought it was a good idea, that's all," said Beany.

"We're close enough to the hide-out anyway," said Sam. "Can't we give the secret signal from here?"

"O.K.," said Matt. "I'll go first." He held the paper whistle against his lips and blew hard. *Beeeeep!* . . . "Black Hawk."

Everything was quiet.

Suddenly, from behind the grapevine, they heard: *Beeeeep!* Then a low voice said, "Golden Tiger."

"Wow-ee!" said Beany "What's that?"

"Something's wrong. There can't be anyone there," Matt whispered. "You try your signal, Sam."

Sam blew his whistle. "Star Fire," he said.

They listened . . .

Once again they heard: *Beeeep!* . . . "Golden Tiger."

"I-I'm getting out of here," said Beany.

"Hold it, Beany!" said Matt. "It's too late to turn back. Give your signal. We'll show him he's outnumbered."

Beany blew his paper whistle weakly. "R-R-Red D-Dragon."

"Come into the secret hide-out, Black Hawk, Star Fire, and Red Dragon," said the voice.

"Come on, you guys," said Matt. "I'm going in. Somebody's in our hide-out, and I'm going to find out who."

Sam stood behind Matt. "Yeah," he said. "Who does he think he is anyway?"

Matt pushed against the tough old grapevines. They wouldn't move. He pushed harder. Suddenly he broke through and fell on his knee. "Ouch!" he said. Then he looked up.

There, right on the side of the hill, was a cave! Just inside the cave, half hidden in a shadow, was a man. He was wearing a lion mask.

"Who's that?" said Matt. "Who are you?"

"I'm scared," whispered Beany. "Who is it?"

"Don't be afraid of your president. Golden Tiger welcomes you to the secret hide-out of the Viking Club," said the man. He slowly lifted the lion mask from his head.

"DAD!" cried Matt and Sam. "It's you!"

"Holy mackerel — it's your father!" said Beany.

"Dad," said Matt, "what are you doing here?"

"I'm Golden Tiger," said Mr. Burns. "And I was president of the Viking Club when I was your age. That's when the secret book was written."

"But how did you know we were trying to become members?" asked Sam.

"Were you spying on us?" said Beany.

"I'll bet I know. He saw us with the secret book at breakfast. Right, Dad?" said Matt.

"I did. That's right," said Mr. Burns.

"We've passed all the tests. Now can we become senior members?" said Matt.

"Yes," said Mr. Burns. "You certainly should be senior members if you've passed the tests."

"Where are the other old members?" said Beany.

"Most of them moved away. I guess they joined other clubs," Mr. Burns said.

"Then this club really needs new members," said Sam. "It's a good thing we found the secret book."

"We brought the secret book with us, Dad. Will you swear us in?" said Matt.

"I'd be honored to," said Mr. Burns.

So Black Hawk, Star Fire, and Red Dragon placed their right hands on the secret book and took the oath of membership.

They swore never to tell anyone where the secret hide-out was. And they never did.

**How to make a
spear, shield, lion mask,
and paper whistle**

How to make a spear

What you need:

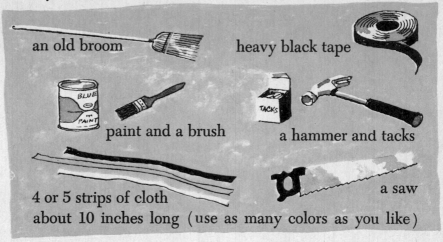

an old broom

heavy black tape

paint and a brush

a hammer and tacks

4 or 5 strips of cloth
about 10 inches long (use as many colors as you like)

a saw

What to do:

1. Cut off the broomstick.

2. Put some heavy black tape around the middle of the broomstick.

3. Paint your spear with a bright color; or use bright-colored tape.

4. This is the way to put the strips of
   cloth on your spear:

   Hold them together like this.

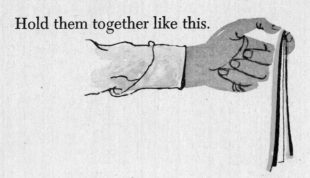

   Put a tack through them.

   Hammer the tack onto the broomstick —
   about 12 inches from the round end.

   Warning: Use the round end of the broomstick for a
   point. Do not sharpen it. A sharp point could
   hurt someone.

How to make a shield

What you need:

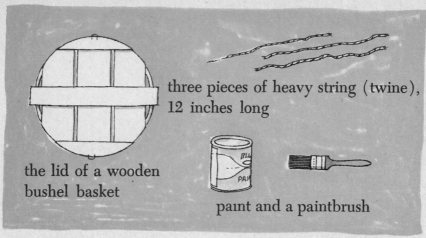

three pieces of heavy string (twine), 12 inches long

the lid of a wooden bushel basket

paint and a paintbrush

What to do:

1. Take one piece of twine and put it between the two large boards in the center of the lid.

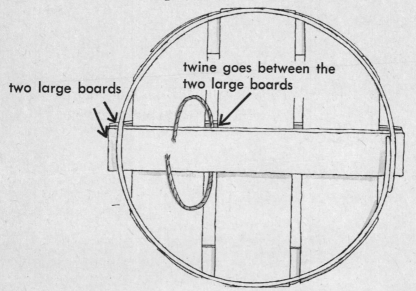

two large boards

twine goes between the two large boards

2. Tie the ends of the twine in a knot. Now you have a circle of twine around the board. You will need three circles of twine. They will make three loops for your arm and your hand.

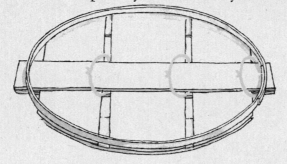

3. Put your arm through two loops and hold one loop with your hand like this.

4. Make a design on your shield with paint or crayons. Here are some ideas. But it is fun to make up your own designs.

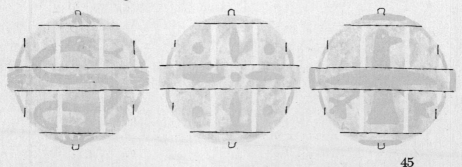

How to make a lion mask

What you need:

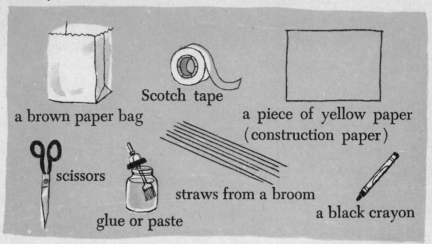

a brown paper bag

Scotch tape

a piece of yellow paper (construction paper)

scissors

glue or paste

straws from a broom

a black crayon

What to do:

1. Put the paper bag over your head. Use a crayon to put a dot where your eyes and mouth are.

2. Take the bag off and draw a scary face on it. For ears, draw a half circle on each side of the bag. Make a dotted line. (Look at the picture to see how to do this.)

3. Now cut holes for the eyes and mouth. Cut along the half circles for ears. Bend the ears out on the dotted line.

bend out

4. Use broom straws to make whiskers. Stick them on with Scotch tape.

5. Draw a zigzag line around three sides of the yellow construction paper. Cut on the line.

6. Glue or paste the yellow paper to the back of the mask. (Look at the picture.) Now the lion has a mane!

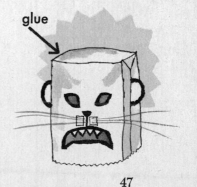

glue

How to make a paper whistle

What you need:

    a small piece of newspaper, 2 inches by 4½ inches

    scissors

What to do:

1. Fold the paper in half.

2. Make two little cuts in the fold.

    cut out here

3. Fold the paper in half again, like this.

4. Open the paper — it should look like this.

5. Now take the two ends and fold them like this.

6. The picture shows you how to hold your whistle. Hold it loosely against your lips. Blow hard!

Be sure there is a *small* space between the two fingers holding the whistle. Remember — air has to go through the diamond-shaped hole.

small space